The Travellers

The first book:
Tess's story

The second book:
Mike's story

The third book:
Lizzie's story

The Travellers: Lizzie
by Rosemary Hayes

Published by Ransom Publishing Ltd.
Unit 7, Brocklands Farm, West Meon, Hampshire GU32 1JN, UK
www.ransom.co.uk

ISBN   978 178127 969 4
First published in 2015

Lizzie

The third book in the series

Rosemary Hayes

Ransom

Acknowledgements

My thanks to everyone who has made time to tell me about the lives of Gypsy/Romany/Travellers, how they live now and how they lived in the past, particularly to those in Cambridgeshire County Council who work with the GRT community and to Gordon Boswell of The Romany Museum, Spalding, Lincolnshire.

I am very grateful to the following members of GRT families who have welcomed me into their homes and talked to me about their experiences:

Brady
Linda
Andrew
Rene
Jessie
Abraham
Abi
and Rita.

The English gypsies I spoke to referred to themselves as either gypsies or travellers, and these terms appear to be interchangeable. Many have Romany roots and still practise some of the old traditions and use words from the Romany language.

Traveller Organisations

The Community Law Partnership (CLP) incorporates the Travellers' Advice Team, a nationwide 24-hour advice service for gypsies and travellers.

The National Federation of Gypsy Liaison Groups

The Gypsy Council

Friends, Families and Travellers

National Association of Gypsy and Traveller Officers

Travellers' Times

The story so far ...

Lizzie is a gypsy girl living with her family on the new council site on the outskirts of the village.

When she first goes to the local primary school she is bullied, but she makes friends with a gorger (non-gypsy) girl in her class called Tess. Tess is pony-mad and she's been helping Lizzie's brother, Mike, look after the gypsy horses – and has got to know Lizzie's family.

Lizzie would like to go to art school, but she knows it's impossible. Her dad won't even let her go on to secondary school and she often has to stay home and look after her younger sister and brother when her mum goes out working as a cleaner.

Lizzie can't believe that Tess has just been to a horse fair without her mum's permission. The two friends haven't seen much of each other lately, what with Lizzie missing school and Tess being banned from going down to the site.

One

It was break time and Lizzie and Tess were sitting in the yard, their backs up against the wall. It was a warm June day and Lizzie held her face up to the sun.

She yawned and stretched. 'You should've told yer mum, Tess. I bet she was mad when she found out.'

Tess hugged her knees. 'Yeah, she was really mad at first, but she's calmed down now.'

She turned towards Lizzie. 'It wasn't being at

the site or being with the horses. It was 'cos I didn't tell her about staying over at the horse fair.'

'So, what's happening? You still grounded?'

Tess shook her head. 'We talked last night. She knows how much I miss Flame – and your family, too.'

'So you can come round again?'

Tess nodded and Lizzie grinned. 'I'm glad.'

Suddenly there was a shout: 'Lizzie!' and both girls looked up to see their form teacher, Mr Hardy, cross the yard and come towards them. As he approached, Lizzie stood up.

'Lizzie,' he said. 'I want to talk to you about something.'

Lizzie frowned nervously, but Mr Hardy was smiling. 'Don't worry, you haven't done anything wrong.'

Tess started to move away.

'Don't go, Tess,' said Mr Hardy, 'You can help with this, too.'

'What's that, sir?'

He opened a file he was holding and drew out a piece of paper.

'I've just been sent this,' he said.

Tess read out the words at the top of the paper. ' "Gypsy, Roma, Travellers' History Month." What's that mean?'

'Just what it says. That this month is special for gypsies. It's Gypsy History Month – and I thought we should do something about it.'

'What sort of thing, sir?' asked Lizzie.

'Well, we've got quite a few traveller children in the school and I think all of us would like to know more about your history – and your traditions.'

'You mean how we used to live?'

'Yes, that, but how you live now, too.'

Tess interrupted. 'Your nan had some great stories about when she was a girl. You could tell some of those.'

'Wait,' said Lizzie. 'I don't want to stand up and talk in front of people. And I don't want kids laughing at us, neither.'

'That won't happen,' said Mr Hardy firmly.

'It would be so great,' said Tess. 'I could help. I could talk about the horses, at least.'

'And the horse fair,' muttered Lizzie.

Tess blushed. 'Yeah. And that.'

'And you wouldn't be doing it on your own,' said Mr Hardy. 'I'll talk to the other traveller kids in the class – and some of your cousins from Year Five could help, too.'

'I dunno, sir. I'm not sure.'

Mr Hardy went on. 'We could have an

exhibition in the school hall – and an assembly, too. It's a great opportunity. Not many schools have the chance to learn about your culture.'

'But what would we say?'

'Tell them what you've told me,' said Tess. 'About how your nan and grandad travelled round and that. The hawking and the fortune-telling and stuff.'

'There's a Romany museum up in Lincolnshire,' said Mr Hardy. 'I'll get onto them and see if they can lend us anything.'

'I think me mam's got a few of Nan's photos still,' said Lizzie slowly.

'Good,' said Mr. Hardy, 'That's settled. I'll talk to the others and then we'll decide how to run the assembly. Meanwhile, Lizzie, you ask your parents if there's anything you can bring in for the exhibition.'

As he was walking away, Lizzie said. 'I never said I'd do it.'

Tess grinned. 'You know what he's like.'

'I'm scared, Tess. There are still kids here who hate us.'

'They're just ignorant. And I bet their families are really boring.'

Lizzie grinned. 'Did you mean it when you said you'd help?'

'Sure.'

As they were walking back to their classroom, Tess said, 'Would your mum come in and talk?'

Lizzie shook her head. 'Nah. Shouldn't think so. She'd not like standing up in front of people.'

Mr Hardy had been busy, and by the end of the day all the primary school kids from the site knew about the traveller exhibition and assembly. Back at the site, though, some of the grown-ups were worried.

'Why do they want to do that? They should leave us be. It'll only stir things up.'

To her surprise, Lizzie found herself defending Mr Hardy's idea.

'The kids only say bad things 'cos they don't know us, don't know about our ways,' she said. 'Mr Hardy's trying to help.'

'Yeah,' said Lizzie's mam. 'He's a good man, that Mr Hardy. He spoke up for us when we first came, didn't he? And he's helped Mike and all.'

A few days later, Mr Hardy told Lizzie how they'd run the assembly.

'We'll get all the traveller children together and have a brainstorming session first,' he said.

'How do you mean, sir?'

'I'll ask you questions about how your folk used to live when they travelled round, how you live now, what customs you still keep, that sort of thing. Then you can prepare the answers before the assembly.'

He told them what the museum had agreed to lend them and Lizzie brought in some photos to show.

Gradually, the exhibition began to take shape. Some of the other families from the site agreed to lend their photos. Lizzie's mum let her borrow the beautiful miniature vardo that her granddad had made.

Mr Hardy picked it up. 'The workmanship in this is amazing, Lizzie. Thank you.'

Before long, there were photos all along the main corridor in the school and the miniature vardo and other ornaments were displayed in the trophy cabinet.

Everyone saw it as they walked to and from their classes – and the parents, too, when they came to collect their children. Often Lizzie would see people staring at the photos, talking about them.

Mr Hardy had asked all the parents to come to the assembly if they could, so the hall was very crowded. Lizzie didn't think many of her family would come, but in the end two of her aunties and lots of the little cousins turned up.

And, right at the last minute, Lizzie's mam had agreed to come and answer questions. Mr Hardy had been to the site and asked her to come. He'd said how helpful it would be. So, for Lizzie's sake, she'd agreed.

Lizzie was standing next to Tess, waiting to be called onto the stage. She glanced over at her mam. When Lizzie's mum saw Tess, she frowned.

'Your mum's still cross with me, isn't she, 'cos I didn't tell Mum about the horse fair?'

'A bit. But she'll be OK if you say you're sorry.'

'Yeah, I will. Anyway, I know you'll both be great,' said Tess. 'And I'll be with you. I'm coming up on the stage too, remember.'

Lizzie giggled. 'They'll think you're a gypsy girl!'

'I'd be proud if they did,' said Tess, squeezing Lizzie's arm.

Two

The assembly started with Mr Hardy saying how the traveller children had been at the school for nearly a year and that they'd fitted in well. Then he mentioned that June was Gypsy, Roma, Travellers' Month and it was a good time to celebrate the Romany culture.

All the traveller kids were up on the stage. And so was Lizzie's mam. And Tess, too. Lizzie's mam was wearing a tartan skirt. 'It's her best,' whispered Lizzie to Tess.

It started awkwardly. Mr Hardy was asking questions, but only got one-word answers. But then he asked about the past, addressing his first question to Lizzie's mam.

'Did your family travel?'

She shook her head. 'No. My folk lived up on a site in the fens and we all worked in the fields. We sometimes went to visit family in other places, but that was our home, the site in the fens.' There was a pause, then she went on.

'But me husband's family went all over. His dad and mam. They followed the work all over the country, setting down on the verges or in farmers' fields.'

'And how did they live?'

Mam smiled. 'My mother-in-law often talked about it. About the freedom of going where you wanted, lighting fires and cooking outside, about the kids sleeping in a tent under the vardo.'

'The vardo?'

'It's a bow-topped van,' chirped up one of the children. 'My nan showed me pictures.'

'And they have them at the fairs,' said another. 'They're all painted.'

Mr Hardy chipped in. 'You've seen the miniature vardo in the display case,' he said to the audience. Then he went on. 'You mention work. What work did your people do, and what do they do now.'

Lizzie could see her mam was getting flustered. 'All sorts,' she said. 'Me husband's dad traded in horses – and me husband still does that.' She glanced across at Tess.

'They've got lovely cobs down the site,' said Tess. 'You should see them in the trotting carts.'

'And we do other stuff. Paving, landscaping, scrap metal, all sorts,' said one of the younger boys.

'Me dad's painting barns for a farmer,' said another.

'So you mostly have your own businesses?' asked Mr Hardy.

'Yes. We work for family. We look out for each other.'

One of the girls in Year Six put up her hand. She was one of the gang that had given Lizzie most grief. 'Do you have big weddings, like that programme on telly?'

Lizzie's mam frowned. 'That were rubbish,' she said angrily. 'We don't live like that. None of my folk could afford a do like that. And as for those lads … '

One of the teachers asked a question. 'You have a strict moral code, is that right?'

'Boys and girls don't mix much,' she said. 'Is that what you mean?'

'What about marriage, then?'

Lizzie looked at her mam. She was struggling, not enjoying being in the limelight.

'We protect our girls,' she said quietly. 'And mostly we marry other gypsies. But not always.'

'And what happens when you marry? Does the girl come to live with the boy's family?'

Mam nodded. 'Mostly that's what happens.' She went on. 'I left my family up in the fens and went to join my husband's folk. At the time, they were on another site not far away.'

'It must have been hard to keep clean, in the old days,' said another teacher.

Lizzie felt herself blushing. Why did people always think gypsies were dirty?

'My nan always kept her van spotless,' she said. 'And she had all these rules about not using bowls for the wrong things.'

'What do you mean?'

'Well, she had a bowl for washing clothes, another for washing up plates and that, and another for washing yourself. She were ever so strict about that.'

The questions began to come thick and fast then. There was a forest of hands going up and Mr Hardy had trouble keeping control.

Lizzie and the others had a job to answer all the questions. They spoke about the life their grandparents had had, hawking round door to door and telling fortunes, about the good times and the bad times. And about how it was now, living on a settled site, with day rooms and showers and kitchens.

'Do many of the gypsy girls ride horses?' asked someone.

Tess answered that one. 'Some. But it's the men who have most to do with them.'

'How come they let you ride, then?' Everyone laughed.

Tess turned to Lizzie. 'I dunno ... I just ... '

'They let her ride 'cos she's brilliant at riding,' said Lizzie, looking across at Tess and smiling.

At last the assembly was over, but for the rest of the day people were talking about it and coming up to Lizzie and the others, asking questions.

'They asked that many questions,' said Lizzie to Tess, when school was over. 'It seemed they were properly interested.'

Mr Hardy was pleased, too. 'Will you thank

your mum for coming, Lizzie. Having her there made a real difference.'

When Mr Hardy walked off, Lizzie said to Tess. 'When are you coming to see us again?'

'I'll come tonight if that's OK? I need to see Mike.'

'What about?'

'Flame – and Angie.'

'Who?'

'Angie, the riding school lady. You've seen her, Lizzie. She's been at the site a few times, looking at Flame, watching her jump and that.'

Lizzie frowned. 'Yeah ... so?'

'She wants me to take Flame over to hers – to the riding school – so we can work on her properly.'

'Can't you do that in our field?'

Tess smiled. 'I could. But there's proper jumps all set up at the riding school, and Angie's there all the time. She could give me lessons ... '

'You'll have to ask me dad. And he's away all summer.'

Tess looked away. 'I thought Mike could ask your dad.'

Lizzie sighed. 'You ain't scared of our men, are you Tess? You've got more words out of Mike than anyone else and you stand up to Dad.'

Tess frowned. 'Your dad's always been fair with me.'

'He likes you. Not many gypsy girls take an interest in the horses – that's mostly men's stuff.' She smoothed her dark hair out of her eyes and started walking towards the school gates.'

'And it helps you're a brilliant rider,' she shouted over her shoulder.

Tess caught her up. 'Did he say that?'

'You know my dad. He don't say much. But I can tell he thinks it.'

Tess blushed. 'I love it, Lizzie. When I'm riding, nothing else matters. All my worries disappear.'

'Huh,' said Lizzie. 'You ain't got much to worry about, girl. You're gonna stay on at school and get some fancy job and earn lots of money.'

Tess heard the resentment. 'You've got your family, Lizzie. Remember, when your nan died, they came from everywhere, didn't they, to be with you. And your cousins and aunties and uncles on the site. I wish I had that.'

When Lizzie said nothing, Tess continued. 'It's just me and mum and Ben most of the time. Mum doesn't get on with her brother and Dad has his new family.'

'Yeah. Family's good, but they all expect you to

be a good gypsy girl and do what gypsy women have always done.'

Is your dad still saying you've got to leave school this term?'

Lizzie nodded.

'Do you *want* to leave?'

Lizzie got up and stretched. 'I dunno. I find the school work hard 'cos I've missed a lot. But I love the art lessons – and the friends. You and Sophie and Tara. I'd really miss me friends. You 'specially.'

'We'll always be friends, Lizzie.'

'You say that Tess, but things change.'

'What do you mean?'

'You'll move on. I'll be stuck at the site minding the kids, then I'll be married and have a load of kids myself. It's just the way it works.'

Tess looked at the ground. 'But you've told me that there are gypsies all over – lawyers and teachers and footballers. Surely you don't have to stay at home. Is that what you want, Lizzie? What about your art?'

Lizzie shrugged. 'Not much use to me, is it? Unless I paint up a wooden vardo or sommat.'

'Don't say that! You've got real talent. You should go to art school, get a job as a designer or illustrator or something.'

'You don't understand,' snapped Lizzie. 'It's hard to break out, do sommat different from the rest. Not many of my family have.'

They walked out of the gates and onto the road.

'What does your mum think?'

'Eh?'

'Does she want you to leave school?'

'She'd like me to have what she never had, but it's the gypsy men that have the last word. She won't go against Dad.'

'She's lovely, your mum.'

Lizzie's face softened. 'She's had a hard life. You heard what she said at assembly. She worked in the fields from when she was little and she had no schooling. We visit her family sometimes, up in the fens. They have it harder up there.'

'What do you mean?'

'This council site we're on down here, it's really good. Not like the site Mam's family's on up there.

'What's it like then?'

'The trailers aren't connected to water pipes and all the toilets and bathrooms and cookers are in a shed across the yard. It's really hard in the winter, there are that many potholes you're always tripping up in the dark, and the kids always have colds.'

'So she's better off down here?'

Lizzie nodded. 'She loves having the day room and the proper shower and cooker. It's a lot easier here, though mind you she still has to work hard, cleaning offices and stuff so we have food on the table.'

'Could she get a better job – not so hard?'

Lizzie looked down at her feet. 'She doesn't mind the cleaning. She's glad of the work. And there's not a lot else she could do, with not being able to read that well.'

'She did get some lessons, then?'

'Not proper lessons. When we were learning to read, she'd ask us to teach her so she could learn her letters, too.'

Lizzie picked up her school bag. 'I'd better get on home,' she said. 'Come round tonight, if you're allowed. I want to show you sommat.'

Lizzie's mum was in the dayroom, watching TV, when Tess arrived.

Tess bit her lip. 'I never had a chance to say sorry,' she said. 'I know I should've told Mum about the horse fair, but I really wanted to go and I was scared she'd stop me.'

Lizzie's mum got up and turned off the TV. She turned to face Tess, her arms folded and her face stern.

'Yes, you should've told her, Tess. I saw her when I was cleaning up at the Tech and I felt really bad about it. I didn't know you'd not told her.'

'Mum didn't blame you!'

Lizzie's mum shook her head. 'No,' she said slowly. 'She's fair, I'll give her that. But she could have, couldn't she? It could've made things difficult.'

Tess hung her head.

'OK, love. We'll say no more about it. Lizzie's over in the van.'

When Tess opened the van door, and peeped inside, she gasped. Lizzie was sitting at the table with a whole lot of brightly coloured pieces of glass spread out in front of her. The sun was shining through the windows, making everything sparkle – the pieces of glass, the china on the side with its gold rims, the little mirrors sewn into the cushions, the crystal vases, the ornate polished picture frames, even the worktops were so clean that they shone.

'What are you doing?'

Lizzie grinned. 'It was Mam's idea,' she said,

and she held out a partly strung necklace. 'What do you think?'

Tess came and sat down at the table and fingered the necklace.

'It's beautiful.'

Lizzie looked pleased. 'Pretty, ain't it? Mam was at a car boot sale and she found all these bits there and then she bought some strong thread and clasps and stuff; she reckoned we could make sommat of them.'

Lizzie had combined all sorts of shapes and colours.

'They're really unusual, Lizzie. You could sell them.'

'Yeah. Hope so.'

Tess picked up a few of the pieces. 'You know Mum would love one of these. She really likes chunky jewellery. Could you make one for her? I'll pay you for it.'

'OK. You pick out what she'd like.'

Tess put a heap of the pieces to one side. Lizzie laughed and shook her head. 'You've not got the eye, Tess. Those won't work together. You leave it to me. I'll make sommat for her.'

'You're a genius. This could be a nice little business for you.'

Lizzie shrugged. 'Well, it's sommat I can do when I'm not minding the kids or cleaning the van,' she said.

'Don't say that.'

'Why not? It's what's going to happen, ain't it?'

Lizzie worked fast, sorting the glass, putting together combinations Tess would never have thought of, head bent over her work in concentration as she threaded the pieces and knotted the ends.

'You could charge proper money for these,' said Tess.

'Well. I'm gonna try them at a car boot sale next weekend. See how they go.'

'What about craft fairs? You'd get a better price.'

'I don't know about that,' muttered Lizzie.

The door of the van opened and Mike put his head round. He frowned when he saw Tess.

'Thought you weren't allowed here,' he said.

'Hi to you, too,' said Tess. 'No. Mum's OK with me coming round again.'

Mike nodded. 'Seen the horses?'

'Yep. I went there first. They're looking good. And Flame ... ' she trailed off.

You gonna start working on the mare now?'

She nodded. 'Yeah, can't wait. And Mike?'

'Yeah?'

'You know Angie?

'Who? Oh you mean the woman from the riding school?'

'Yeah.'

Lizzie chipped in. 'She wants Tess to take the mare over there, so they can work on her properly like.'

Mike rounded on Lizzie. 'You suddenly an expert, are you?'

'Don't talk to her like that!'

'She's me sister. I'll talk to her how I like.'

Lizzie put a warning hand on Tess's arm.

Tess cleared her throat. 'I could do a lot more with her over there, Mike. And get proper instruction – about the jumping,' she added quickly.

'Me dad won't like it if the mare goes away,' he said.

'Could you ask him?'

'I'll think about it.'

Three

Lizzie's mam came over later. She sat beside Lizzie, watching her work. Occasionally she would pick up a colourful piece of glass and hold it up to the light. The skin on her hands was coarse and red.

Lizzie smiled at her. 'What d'you think?'

'You've got a real eye, love. Like my gran. She could make anything out of nothing.' She sat back, her hands idle in her lap. 'And me granddad, too. He made clothes pegs and skewers and wooden flowers and your nan decorated wooden spoons, made candles from fat, and she made lucky charms from bark and she hawked ribbon and lace and such, sold it door to door.'

'Where did she get the lace and ribbons?'

'Oh she'd buy it cheap from the warehouses and sell it on for a few pence profit. And bunches of white heather for luck and bunches of wild flowers, too. She'd pick snowdrops and bunch them up prettily. She was a real hard worker.'

'So are you, Mam.'

'Different sort of work, love. There's no call for the door-to-door selling now. Everything's changed.'

Lizzie held up two matching strands of wire-threaded glass. She bent the wire at the top of each and handed them to her mam.

'Try 'em.'

Her mam threaded them carefully through her pierced ears.

Lizzie clapped her hands. 'They suit you. Keep them!'

'No, love. You sell them. Be a hawker, like your nan.'

They sat together for a few moments in silence, then Lizzie stretched and yawned.

'It must have bin hard for her in them days. For her and granddad,' she said.

'It's always bin hard for us gypsies,' said Mam. 'Though it's good here, ain't it? We're warm and we can keep clean really easily.'

Lizzie picked up a half-finished necklace. 'You know when you said your gran slept under the wagon when she was little?'

'Umm.'

'How did that work? Wasn't it ever so cold?'

'She said it weren't bad. They had a big layer of straw or reeds, then a sheet spread on top of that, so it weren't damp, then a bender tent over the top.'

'They had a barrel-top wagon, didn't they?'

Mam nodded. 'Gran's brothers were carpenters. They made the wagon for her and me grandad.'

Lizzie nodded. 'I've seen pictures. It were beautiful. Same as Little Nan's dad and mum's. Pity they got burnt.'

Mam shifted in her seat. 'It were the custom, love. You know that. You burn the dead person's belongings. Or bury them.'

'But you wouldn't do that now, would you?'

Mam thought for a moment. 'No. Some Romany folk still do, but I don't believe in it.'

'But you buried Little Nan with all her jewellery.'

Mam shrugged. 'It was what she wanted. And your dad said he wouldn't feel right passing it on.'

Lizzie wondered if she could have used some of Little Nan's jewellery to sell on, but then she dismissed the thought. If Nan had wanted to be buried with it, that was her business. She tied another knot and snipped off the ends with scissors.

'We've still got her pots, though.'

Mam nodded, smiling. 'And me mam's baking pot and cooking pot, too.'

She sighed. 'When I was a girl up in the fens, we had lovely broths and me mam would make Sunday cakes. And we ate a lot of rabbit and pheasant. Our dogs would catch them.'

'Your dad bred dogs, didn't he?'

'Yes. Lurchers. Lovely things they were. I grew up with them.'

She fingered a bracelet Lizzie had just finished. 'They got by, me mam and dad' she said. 'And they never took a penny from the Government.'

'I wish I'd known them,' said Lizzie.

'Me dad was a tough man, but he had a soft side, too. He would have loved you. He used to play the fiddle. He could pick up any tune and in the summer we'd sit out round the fire and some of the grown-ups would dance.'

'It sounds great,' said Lizzie. But she wasn't really concentrating.

'Sometimes it was great,' said Mam. 'But sometimes it were horrible.'

Her mam's voice had changed and Lizzie looked up, frowning.

'Cold and wet in the winter. Kids always getting sick. And the abuse we got, Lizzie. I tell you, it were a lot worse than what we get now. Bailiffs raiding our camps at dawn, forcing us off the land, locals throwing stones at us, calling us names, saying we were dirty.'

Mam's face was set and she was frowning.

'It's still happening, Mam,' said Lizzie quietly.

'Not like it was, girl. Look at you. You've made friends with gorger kids, Tess and Tara and Sophie. I never had friends outside. All my friends were gypsy kids, family mostly. That's why not many of us marry outside. Gorgers don't understand us, don't understand our customs.'

Lizzie stopped working, her hands still, and suddenly the hopelessness of it all overwhelmed her and she saw her future stretching out before her.

'What's the matter love? You're crying.'

Lizzie sniffed and wiped her eyes with the back of her hand.

'Is that how it's going to be for me, Mam? You

gonna find me some nice gypsy boy when I'm seventeen?'

Her mam put her arm round Lizzie's shoulders.

'It's not what I want, Mam. You know it's not.'

'Not all gypsy boys are like your dad, Lizzie.'

Lizzie was shocked. Mam had never said anything like this to her before.

She chose her words carefully. 'I love me dad, Mam, but he's living in the past.'

'I know. But he wants to protect you. He doesn't want you getting friendly with fast gorger girls. And he doesn't want you to mix with gorger boys when you're older.'

'Tess isn't fast, Mam!'

Mam smiled. 'Tess is different. He tolerates her 'cos she's good with the horses. And she saved the mare and foal, too.'

'He's scared, isn't he?'

Her mam frowned. 'Scared?'

Lizzie nodded. And suddenly she felt really sorry for her dad. Like Mam, he worked so hard to help feed and clothe his family, but the world was changing around him and he couldn't keep up. No wonder he lashed out sometimes.

Lizzie went on. 'It's 'cos he had no schooling. He thinks we can get by without much schooling, too.

But we can't, not now. If we want to move on … '

'He's agreed to let Mike stay on, but … ' She hesitated. 'He thinks it's different for girls.'

'Oh Mam,' said Lizzie, looking up to the ceiling of the van. 'If only he could move with the times. Like you.'

Mam laughed. 'Me!'

'Yes. You understand.'

'I understand you want to better yourself, Lizzie, get some qualifications, but getting your dad to agree, that's another thing.'

There was some yelling going on outside the van and it brought Mam up short.

'Those kids,' she said. 'I'd better go and give them their tea. Then I must go to work.'

'Mam?'

'Umm.'

'Could you do one of your rasher puddings in the big pot on the open fire? It's ages since we had one.'

Mam smiled. 'Sure.'

'And p'raps I could get Tess and the others to come?'

Mam hesitated for a moment. 'Yes. Why not.'

When she'd gone, Lizzie sat still, thinking. She'd never had a talk like that with her mam before.

She looked round the van, sparkling clean. She thought of her mam's rough hands, polishing and wiping, keeping it all immaculate, and then saw the beautifully carved miniature vardo. Lots of people at school had admired it. She picked it up and looked at it, all in proportion and painted with bright colours. That would have been Mam's granddad, too, she supposed. She'd never asked.

So the artistic stuff all came from her mam's family, then?

But the gift to see into the future, that was from her dad's side, from her little nan. She shivered suddenly and started to put away all the pieces of jewellery.

She didn't want to think about that gift. It scared her.

Four

At school the next day, Lizzie was quiet, the chatter from Tess, Tara and Sophie drifting over her head. They were talking about a school trip.

'You coming on the trip, Lizzie?' asked Sophie.

Lizzie frowned. 'You know I'm not,' she said crossly.

'She's not allowed,' said Tess. 'You know that, Soph.'

'But why not, Lizzie. What's the harm in it?'

Lizzie sighed. 'I've told you a hundred times. My folk don't like it.'

'Why not?'

Tess could see that Lizzie was getting cross. 'Leave it, Soph. It's just how it is.'

Then she went on to talk about Flame. The horses didn't interest Lizzie and she tuned out. So did Tara and Sophie, so eventually Tess shut up.

'Hey. Only three more weeks of school. Then we're out of here. Up to big school next year ... ' Tara punched the air. 'The village college.'

'I'm SO ready for it,' said Tess.

'Me too,' said Sophie, grinning. Then her smile faded when she saw Lizzie's expression.

'D'you think your dad will let you come on to the village college?'

'Doubt it. He wants me at home to mind the kids and cook and clean,' she said bleakly.

There was an awkward silence.

'And marry some nice gypsy boy when I'm seventeen.'

'Cool,' said Tara. 'Will you have one of those huge wedding dresses like on that telly programme?'

Lizzie's eyes flashed. 'That programme was rubbish,' she said. 'You heard what Mam said at assembly. We don't live like that. You know we don't.'

'Sorry,' said Tara. 'I didn't mean … '

Lizzie's temper subsided as quickly as it had flared. 'No, I know you understand how we live. It just makes me so mad when they show sommat like that on the telly. It's done so much harm and it makes everyone hate us.'

Tess came up and put her arms round Lizzie's shoulders. 'We all love you, girl,' she said. She turned to the others. 'You should see the jewellery she's making. It's fantastic!'

'Wow! Will you bring some into school?'

Lizzie shook her head. 'No. I wouldn't do that. But you can come round the site and see it.'

Sophie clapped her hands. 'Great! When?'

Lizzie smiled. 'Tell you what. Why don't you all come over on the weekend and I'll get Mam to cook her bacon pudding over the fire outside. It's great when we sit round the fire and yarn and that. And Mam might get some of the others to come. One of me uncles plays the mouth organ, and one of me cousins plays the penny whistle and the accordion.'

'That sounds great,' said Sophie. 'Count me in.'

But later on, out of Lizzie's earshot, Tara and Sophie came up to Tess.

'Will it be OK? Will it be safe?'

Tess rolled her eyes. 'Of course it's safe, you idiots. They all know me and I'll be with you.'

At the weekend Lizzie helped her mam make the rasher puddings, rolling out the pastry, laying the onion, bacon and potatoes on it and then carefully rolling it all up and wrapping it in muslin, tied at the ends.

They built a fire outside and hung a pot of water over it to boil. The younger kids ran round in excitement and the smell of cooking wafted up into the still air.

'It's a lovely day for it,' said Mam, squinting into the sunlight. She wiped her hands on her apron and smiled.

'This was when it was good,' she said. 'In the summer.' She went on. 'You know your little nan really missed the outdoor life. She used to say there was nothing better. The freedom. Being able to go from place to place when you wanted.'

Lizzie looked up. 'Is that what you'd want, Mam? Would you want to travel round?'

Mam laughed. 'It's in our blood isn't it? We're always wanting to move on. But we're lucky here. It's a good place. And we're warm in the winter. On days like this you forget how it was in the winter.'

Lizzie waited for the others at the entrance to the site. She knew Tess was already at the field, riding Flame. Tess was often here and everyone knew her, but Sophie and Tara had only been a couple of times and they'd never eaten with her family. She felt nervous.

They were all awkward at first, but the ice was broken when Tara took a small package out of her pocket and handed it to Lizzie's mum.

'Tess says you like china,' she said, blushing.

Mam opened the package. Inside was a small, heavily decorated dish edged with gold.

'Oh, it's lovely! It's really lovely!' She held it close to her chest. 'Thank you, love.'

Her pleasure was so genuine that both Sophie and Tara relaxed. Tara was relieved. Her own mum had been going to throw out the dish, saying it was too flashy.

They sat round the fire, the wood smoke stinging their eyes. A few minutes later, Tess joined them.

'Phew!' said Sophie. 'You stink of horses!'

Tess grinned. 'Goes with the territory,' she said. 'And anyway, it's a great smell.'

'If you say so,' said Tara, holding her nose.

When the rasher puddings were ready, Lizzie and her mum took them out of the water and set them to drain, before taking off the muslin cloths and slicing them up.

Mike, Johnny and the younger children all ate with them. Neither of the bigger boys spoke to Sophie and Tara, but Tess talked to Mike about the horses and the younger children rushed about laughing and yelling.

After they'd eaten and were sitting round the dying embers of the fire, one of Lizzie's uncles joined them and started playing a few tunes on his mouth organ. Later, one or two others drifted over. Another man had an accordion.

There was nothing formal about the music but it blended beautifully and, as the evening wore on, someone stoked the fire and more relations came over, chatting together, laughing, drinking beer and singing.

Tess touched Lizzie's arm. 'You're lucky,' she said.

'Eh?'

'To have all this.'

Lizzie smiled. 'Yeah, I s'pose.' Then she turned to Sophie and Tara. 'D'you want to come and look at the jewellery?'

She took the girls into the van. Every spare moment, Lizzie'd been making up the jewellery and she had the pieces spread out across the table.

'You've been busy!' said Tess. 'You've done masses since I saw it.'

Lizzie nodded. 'I like doing it,' she said simply.

Sophie and Tara stared. 'Lizzie,' breathed Sophie. 'These are really special. You're brilliant!'

Lizzie blushed. 'Glad you like them.'

'What are you going to do with them? You should sell them.'

Lizzie nodded. 'There's a car boot sale coming up.'

'I told her she should sell them at a craft fair or something. She'd get a better price.'

'Tell you what,' said Tara. 'Why don't you take a stall at the school fair?'

'But that's this Friday.'

'So? You've got enough to sell haven't you?'

Lizzie frowned. 'Isn't the fair to raise money for the school?'

'Yeah, but I think you just pay for a pitch. I don't think it's much.'

'More than I can afford,' said Lizzie.

'But think, Lizzie,' said Sophie. 'You could make the stall really special, decorate it. She looked round the van and gestured to the curtains. 'You could drape it with stuff like that, all sparkly and lovely.'

Lizzie looked thoughtful. 'Mam's got some shawls – and maybe she'd let me borrow the curtains.'

'A gypsy stall,' cried Tara, clapping her hands. 'How cool would that be?'

Lizzie bit her lip. 'I dunno … '

'We'll help you,' said Tess, 'with getting the stall ready and price labels and stuff.'

'But aren't you all going on the school trip next week?'

'Oh. Oh yeah, I'd forgotten.'

'We don't leave till Tuesday,' said Tara. 'And it's only two days. We'll be back Thursday.'

'Hang on,' said Lizzie, laughing. 'We don't know if I can have a stall yet. And how much it is.'

But the others were fired up. 'We'll ask tomorrow. We'll find out how much it costs to hire a pitch.'

When they left, Lizzie carefully put away the pieces she'd made, examining each one in turn with a critical eye.

Yes. They were OK. She was pleased with them. She hugged herself and sighed. Maybe this would

work. Maybe other people would want to buy
them.

    Maybe.

Five

Lizzie helped her mam get the little ones off to bed, then she joined her by the fire. It had died right down now, but the smell was still there, hanging in the air, the smell of wood smoke.

It was good to have Mam around in the evening. Weekends were special like that. Every other evening she was out cleaning.

'Come and sit for a bit, Lizzie.'

The boys and the other relations had disappeared and they were alone together.

Lizzie told her mam about the school fair.

'That's a great idea,' said Mam.

'You don't mind?'

''Course not. It'd be better than a car boot sale.'

'What would Dad say?'

Mam laughed. 'Your dad? If you can make a bit of money, love, he'd be all for it!'

'But what if it costs too much to book the pitch?'

Mam hesitated. 'It can't be that much, can it?'

'Dunno. I'll find out.'

'You do that, love. We'll manage somehow.'

At school the next day, Tess, Tara, Sophie and Lizzie went to find the teacher organising the fair.

'Oh I don't know, Lizzie. I'd like to say yes but we're pretty full up. I'm not sure we could fit in another stall.'

'But miss,' said Sophie. 'You should see what she's made. It's really great.'

'Show her, Lizzie,' said Tess.

The teacher looked at her watch. 'Well, all right, but I have to go in a minute. Quickly, then.'

Lizzie had brought a few samples with her and she handed them over.

The teacher looked at them, turning them over in her hands.

'Hey, these are beautifully made, Lizzie. Really unusual. I didn't know you were so talented. We must certainly have these in the fair. It will be a bit of a tight fit, but I'm sure we can find a space for you somewhere.'

Lizzie cleared her throat. 'How much do I have to pay for it, miss?'

'Oh, the pitch fee is £15,' said the teacher, then she looked at her watch again. 'I really must go now. I'll make sure you have a table, dear. Come along to the hall at lunch time on Friday when we're setting up. You can bring the money then, too.'

As the teacher walked away, Tara punched the air. 'Result!'

Lizzie grinned. 'Thanks guys. It was all your idea.'

'What about the money?' said Tess.

Lizzie frowned. 'I think it'll be OK. Mam's all for it. She'll help me out and I should get the money back from selling the stuff.'

Tess squeezed her arm. 'Of course you will. It's gorgeous.'

'What should I charge?'

'Don't under price it, Lizzie,' said Tara. 'Think of all the hours you've spent making it.'

'I suppose,' said Lizzie. 'And Mam had to pay a bit for the beads and glass bits and thread and clasps.'

'Well, there you are.'

'They'll be a lot of parents there. It's not just the kids spending their pocket money.'

By the end of the day, Lizzie and the others had decided on prices for most of the pieces. Lizzie totted up what her mam had spent and the pitch fee and took all that off from what she'd make if she sold every single piece.'

'You're ever so good at figures, Lizzie,' said Tara.

Lizzie laughed. 'That's gypsies for you,' she said. 'We may not be so good at the reading and writing, but we can always count the money. We always know the value of things.'

'You should make a good profit,' said Sophie.

'Well, if I sell everything I will. But if I don't it won't look so clever.'

That evening she started thinking about her stall. She wanted it to stand out, be different from the others. She'd been to school fairs before. Mostly stuff just laid out on tables, cakes and people's casts-off and tatty things made by the kids. She wanted a back to her stall so she could drape a cloth over it, and she wanted to show off each piece of jewellery properly. She experimented by putting stones underneath a cloth and spreading each piece of jewellery on top. She was so busy that she didn't notice the time.

Mam came into the van. 'We need to get the kids to bed, love. You'd best clear up your bits.' Then she stopped. 'That's a great idea, displaying them like that. They look lovely.'

'I want to put summat at the back of the stall, too, Mam. So it looks different from the others.'

Her mam thought for a bit, then she smiled. 'I know just what you can do,' she said.

Most of her form were on the school trip, with just Lizzie and a few others left behind. It was so near the end of term that no one made them do much work and Lizzie was able to spend time in the art room. She explained her plan to the art teacher.

'It was me mam's idea,' said Lizzie. 'D'you think it would work?'

'Of course it will work. We'll make it work.'

Lizzie really liked her art teacher. From the start, she'd encouraged her, praised her work.

'I'm really excited about this, Lizzie. Come on, let's see what there is in the storeroom.'

They dug around in the art cupboard.

'I know we've got some somewhere,' said the art teacher. 'I think they are right at the back.' She pushed more stuff out of the way. 'Yes! Here we are.'

She backed out holding several huge pieces of card.

'Look. We can use these, put struts behind so they stay up, then you can paint the card.'

The art teacher got busy with the staple gun, attaching the cards to the struts, and before long they had a sturdy freestanding structure. They stood back to admire their work.

'How are you going to decorate it?'

'Lots of bright colours, pictures of the jewellery. That sort of thing. And maybe a few scarves draped over the ends.'

'What about a title?'

'A title?'

'For your stall. You could call it *Lizzie's Jewellery*.'

'Umm. Maybe.'

Lizzie was allowed to spend most of the next two days working on her project. She took endless trouble over it, painting pictures of the necklaces and bracelets, earrings and rings on a background that really showed them up. At last she'd finished it and she showed it to the art teacher.

'Fantastic, Lizzie! Well, if that doesn't get them flocking to your stall, nothing will.'

Lizzie went home that night really excited. Tess, Tara and Sophie would be back tomorrow. She couldn't wait to show them what she'd done. And she couldn't wait to put up her stall at lunch time.

It wasn't until break time that they could all go into the art room.

'Close your eyes,' demanded Lizzie.

She went over to the corner. The backdrop had its blank side towards her and she turned it round.

'OK, you can look now.'

But, instead of the oohs and ahhs she'd hoped for, there was a shocked silence.

She looked at her friends – and then she looked at the backdrop.

Her hand flew to her mouth and she blushed crimson.

It was supposed to say *Lizzie's Jewellery*, but *Lizzie's* had been crossed out with red paint and in its place, in more red paint, still wet, was written *Gypsy*.

'Oh Lizzie!'

Lizzie started to cry. 'Why would anyone do that? Why do they hate me?'

All four girls stared at it in silence, then Tara cleared her throat.

'It's still great, Lizzie. You can still use it.'

'What! shouted Lizzie, 'With that scrawled all over it.'

'No, listen, Lizzie,' said Tess. 'Tara's right. 'You're not ashamed of being a gypsy, are you?'

'Of course I'm not. You know that. It's just … '

'Well then, you should show this idiot up. Show them you're proud of who you are.' She smiled. 'Anyway I think *Gypsy Jewellery* sounds pretty good.'

Lizzie sniffed and wiped her nose on the back of her hand.

'It's jealousy. 'Cos you're so brilliant,' said Sophie.

The art teacher came into the room. She gasped when she saw what had happened.

'That is dreadful. I'm going to find out who did this. It's vandalism.' She went up to Lizzie. 'Look love, I can probably get most of the red paint off.

I've got some solvents … '

But suddenly Lizzie stood up straight and put back her shoulders.

'D'you know what. The girls are right. Let's leave it there. I am a gypsy. And I'm proud of it.'

The art teacher looked at her for a moment, then she laughed. 'You are so right, Lizzie. It's not your problem, it's *theirs*.'

Six

Lizzie and the art teacher worked on the backdrop a bit more. By the time the display was up in the main hall, *Gypsy Jewellery* looked as if it had always been the title. Lizzie stood back and squinted at it.

'Yeah. It looks good,' she said.

'More than good,' said Tess. 'It looks amazing. It's definitely the best stall in the place.'

As soon as school was over, the fair was opened and families flocked into the hall. Lizzie's mam came, with the younger children.

'It's the best stall here,' she whispered.

Lizzie smiled at her. Mam had made an effort. She'd put on some make-up and her best skirt.

'You look great, Mam.'

Sophie was nearby. 'She's right,' she said. 'You look fantastic!'

As more people arrived, the space round Lizzie's stall became crowded. People fingered the jewellery, picked it up and looked at it and there were lots of comments.

'Really unusual.'

'Such lovely colours.'

'Could wear this with anything.'

And it wasn't long before the first piece sold. Tess had offered to help with the selling, but there was no need. Lizzie was quick to give change and she even had some sheets of coloured tissue paper that she used to wrap the pieces, twisting the ends so that the jewellery stayed inside.

Her mam smiled. That had been her idea. She'd kept all the old paper that Little Nan had used to make paper flowers. Nan would have been pleased that it was being used.

There was a group of girls standing by at the edge of the stall. Lizzie saw them but she said nothing. One of them picked up a pair of earrings and turned to the others. 'It's very pricey for such a bit of tat,' she said.

One of the mums overhead what she said and rounded on her.

'There's real skill in that,' she said. 'And you'd pay much more for it in a shop.' She turned to Lizzie. 'I think you've priced them very reasonably, love.'

When there was a quiet moment, Lizzie whispered to Tess. 'That girl who said my stuff was tat ... ' She pointed to the group of girls who had moved off and were lurking round another stall. 'I think it was her that daubed the paint.'

'She's not in our form. Do you know her?'

Lizzie nodded. 'She's in my special reading class. She and her mates are always giving me grief.'

'Well. You've shown her, haven't you?' Tess looked at the nearly empty stall. 'You've almost sold out and there's still another hour to go.'

Lizzie smiled. 'Thanks girls. You've been great.'

Tess gave Lizzie a hug. 'We'll go and have a look round then we'll come back and help you clear up,' she said.

When the fair closed, Lizzie's stall was empty. Everything had sold and she was counting out the money.

When Tess and the others came back, her eyes

were shining. 'I've made a tidy profit,' she said. 'Even with all the expenses.'

'You deserve it,' said Tara. 'You've worked really hard.'

'OK, super saleswoman, what do you want us to do?'

'Wait,' said Lizzie, bending down and picking something up from under the table. 'Just before we clear up, I've got something for you.'

She was holding three packages, all different shapes, all wrapped in brightly coloured tissue paper.

'Yellow for Tara,' she said, handing one over, 'Blue for Sophie. Red for Tess.'

The girls opened their presents.

'Wow!' said Sophie, holding up a delicate necklace of blue stones. 'That's lovely, Lizzie.' She immediately put it round her neck and the others admired it.

'It really suits you. The colour's just right. You're so clever, Lizzie.'

Lizzie smiled. 'Well, it's sommat I can do,' she said. 'And you've bin good friends to me.'

When Tess opened her present, Lizzie watched her. 'Yours is a bit different,' she said. 'I hope you like it.'

Tess weighed the package in her hand. It was

quite heavy. Carefully she unwrapped it and held up a bracelet. It was made of black and read beads and over the clasp there was a little brass horse's head.

'Oh Lizzie, that's fantastic!' She held it up and turned it round and round.

'I love it. Where did the little horse's head come from?'

'It was Little Nan's,' she said. 'She gave it to me just before she died. I thought you'd like it 'cos you used to talk to her about the old days.'

Tess hugged Lizzie and there were tears in her eyes. 'I loved your nan,' she said. 'I'll wear it all the time. It'll be my lucky bracelet.'

The art teacher helped them put away the back drop in the art room.

'You can take that up to the college next term Lizzie,' she said. 'They have an exhibition every year there. You could use it again.' She went on. 'They have a lovely art department. And a proper trained art teacher.'

'I won't be going to the college, miss,' said Lizzie quietly.

There was silence and suddenly all the excitement of the day drained away. She didn't want to leave school. She didn't want to be stuck on the site minding the kids and cleaning and cooking. She sighed and turned away. The art teacher had started talking again, but she didn't hear what she was saying.

'Lizzie, you're not listening.'

'Sorry miss.'

'I said, is your mother waiting for you?'

Lizzie nodded. 'Yeah. She's driving me back in the van, then she's got to go out to work.'

'Good. I'd like a word with her.'

Lizzie frowned. If the teacher was going to try and persuade Mam to let Lizzie stay on at school, she'd get nowhere. It wasn't Mam she needed to convince. It was Dad.

Lizzie picked up all the scarves and material and the stones and put them carefully into bags. She said goodbye to Tess, Tara and Sophie, then the art teacher helped her carry the bags out to the school yard. Mam was waiting in the beaten-up old van, the kids running round outside it. She could see Mam was anxious. She'd not want to be late for work.

The art teacher smiled at her. 'Lizzie's done really well with her stall,' she said, as she helped put the bags in the back of the van. 'Everything sold.'

'That's great, love. Now you hop in. We'd best get going.'

'Just before you go.' The art teacher took a poster out of her pocket and smoothed it open. 'There's something I want to show you.'

Mam frowned. Lizzie could sense her unease. Mam's reading was slow and it took her a long time to figure words out.

Lizzie took the poster. 'What's this, miss?'

'It's a competition, Lizzie. And I think you should enter it.'

Lizzie frowned. She made out the words *County Art Competition*.

'What sort of competition?' asked Mam.

'It's a big one. All the schools in the county are going to enter.'

'And you think our Lizzie should do a picture?'

'Yes. Why not?'

Lizzie handed the poster back. 'I'm not good enough for that, Miss.'

The art teacher pushed the poster back into Lizzie's hands.

'Just think about it Lizzie. There's no rush. The entries don't have to be in until next term.'

'Sorry I'm late, Mam,' said Lizzie, as she climbed into the van. 'I couldn't get away, what with packing the stall away.'

'You did ever so well, love. I'm proud of you.

And I'm glad you called your stall *Gypsy Jewellery*.'

Lizzie smiled to herself. Mam went on. 'The kids had sommat to eat while we waited, but you'll have to put them to bed, love.'

As they drove under the motorway bridge, Lizzie glanced at the graffiti painted there. A couple of her cousins had done it and it wasn't bad. Pictures of old vardos and horses and a big 'Welcome' sprawled across the top.

Mam dropped them at the site and then drove off to work. The kids were over-excited and Lizzie couldn't get them to settle.

I really don't need this!

One of her aunties heard the noise and came into the van to help. When at last the youngsters were in bed, she and her auntie sat on the steps of the van and shared some food. After she'd eaten and her auntie had left, Lizzie leaned back against the van and looked up into the evening sky.

Nearly the end of term. Nearly the end of her school life.

She thought about the school fair. She'd loved it. Loved showing off her jewellery, loved the hustle and bustle of selling it. Loved everything about it. Maybe she'd make more during the summer, go round picking up stuff at car boot sales.

Dad wouldn't mind that, would he? Bartering, trading, hustling. That's what gypsies did, wasn't it? Perhaps he'd be glad if she built up a little business and hawked her stuff round to fairs.

She yawned and stretched. She'd go to bed early. It had been a long day. She counted out her money and put it in a special tin. Although she'd often helped Mam and the rest of her family at car boot sales, it was the first time she'd earned anything for herself.

As she was undressing, she felt the crackle of the poster, crumpled up in her pocket. She got it out and smoothed it open. She looked at it for a long time, reading about how to enter.

You had to give your name and the name of your school. But she wouldn't have a school next term.

Anyway, Dad wouldn't like it if she entered the competition. He was suspicious of things like that.

She sighed. There were that many clever kids around, it wasn't as if she'd win a prize or anything.

She folded up the poster and put it away.

Seven

Just before the end of term, a lady from the council came into school to talk to all the traveller kids in Year Six. She told them how important it was to keep on with school, to go on to the village college and finish their education.

'They have courses at the school,' said the lady. 'Not just academic courses. You can begin learning a trade there, too, then you could go on to the Tech.'

Some of the others looked quite interested. 'What sort of classes, miss?'

She handed out a leaflet. Lizzie took one. She was right, there was lots of stuff; hairdressing, beauty therapy and so on.

'What if you don't go on to the village college, miss?'

Lizzie looked up. The girl who had asked the question was one of her cousins. Her dad was against girls going on to secondary school, too.'

'Then there's home schooling.' The lady handed out more leaflets.

'You have to keep on with your schooling,' she said. 'It's the law.'

She droned on about some home education pack, about tutors coming to visit travelling families.

Lizzie stopped listening. It wouldn't work. Not if your mam and dad couldn't help you. She'd known older kids on the site have home education. The tutors didn't visit that often, the kids never bothered to do work on their own and their parents weren't interested.

Though there were some who managed. She frowned. Another cousin – Lala – she'd been home educated and she'd got a good job now. But then Lala's mum was really clever. She'd campaigned for gypsy rights and all sorts.

She sighed. Maybe she'd talk to Lala's mum.

When the lady from the council had finished, all the gypsy kids from Year Six went back to their classroom. Lizzie noticed the gang in the back row sniggering as she and the others walked in. She wasn't in the mood for their teasing, so she gave them a death stare and went and sat next to Tess.

At break, the gang came up to her.

'You going somewhere nice on holiday, Lizzie?' said one, innocently.

Lizzie didn't answer.

'She's gonna stay on that smelly site,' said another, giggling.

'And you're not going on the college, are you? 'Cos your daddy wants you to stay home in your poxy van and mind the kids.'

Lizzie felt her anger rising. They were only getting at her because she was on her own. If Tess or Sophie or Tara had been with her they wouldn't dare talk like that. She clenched her fists but said nothing.

Hadn't they learnt anything? They were never going to understand. All that effort at assembly had been a waste of time.

'Was that your mother at assembly?' said one.

'Not got much fashion sense, has she?'

'Did you see all that tatty bling she was wearing?' said another.

She didn't know why she snapped. She'd been got at before, mostly by the same group of girls, but suddenly everything got to her. They were right. She wouldn't be going anywhere on holiday and they were right about her staying home to mind the kids, but it was when they started on her mam …

She lashed out. It was so sudden and unexpected that she already had two of them on the ground before they realised, and was hitting and scratching, pulling their hair.

One of the others screamed. 'Quick! Miss! Over here. The gypsy girl is killing them.'

It was over in a matter of seconds. Two members of staff ran over and pulled Lizzie off the girls.

Then Mr Hardy was there – and Tess.

Tess put her arm round Lizzie. Lizzie started to cry. 'They were saying stuff about my mam,' she gulped.

The two girls were on their feet again. 'She hit us sir. And she scratched us. She's a bloody cat!'

'That's enough,' said Mr Hardy. 'Go to my office now.' Then he turned to Lizzie. 'I'm disappointed in you, Lizzie. I know what you've had to put up with, but violence is never the answer.'

Lizzie was still crying. 'I'm sorry sir, I didn't mean to. I just couldn't hack it any more.'

Mr Hardy sighed. 'I'll see you in my office at lunch time.'

Lizzie nodded miserably.

'Bitches!' said Tess. 'Don't take any notice of them, Lizzie. They're jealous, that's all. They've got nothing in their sad little lives and they're taking it out on you.'

'But it was right, what they said. Not the stuff about Mam, but the other stuff, about not going on to college and not going on any fancy holiday. '

'Well I'm not going on any fancy holiday either,' said Tess.

'You'll be at the riding school all the time.'

'Well, I will if I can take Flame over there,' said Tess. 'But you've got your jewellery, Lizzie. You can make more and sell it over the summer. There's local fêtes, and fairs and stuff.'

'I s'pose.'

'And what about the horse fairs? They'd go well there, wouldn't they?'

'Mam wouldn't let me go to the horse fairs,' said Lizzie. 'And anyway, the boys wouldn't want me hanging around.'

They were quiet for a bit, then Tess said,

'I haven't seen Mike for a bit. Has he asked your dad if I can take Flame over to the riding school?'

'I dunno. I don't think so. He's that busy. I daren't ask him. He's always tired and grumpy. He's helping me uncle in the gardening business every weekend, then he's got school work.'

'When's the next horse fair?'

'There was a big one last month. They didn't go to that one. But there's a couple more in the summer and then another couple in the autumn.'

'I'd really like to go to another one,' said Tess. 'But after last time … '

'No,' said Lizzie, smiling. 'Best not.'

They made their way back to the classroom. 'Only one more day of school,' said Tess.

'Yeah,' said Lizzie. 'My last day at school ever.'

'Oh Lizzie!'

She shrugged. 'Can't be helped.'

'I'll wait for you at lunch time, when you go and see Mr Hardy.'

'Thanks.'

The office door was open and Mr Hardy was inside, peering out of his window.

'Come in and sit down, Lizzie,' he said.

'I'm sorry sir,' she said. 'I dunno why I lost it like that. I know I didn't ought ... '

He held up his hand. 'I know you were provoked, Lizzie. And I know you're sorry. We'll say no more about it – OK?'

She nodded.

Mr Hardy turned round to face her. 'But right now, I want to talk about your future, Lizzie.'

She stared glumly at her feet. 'I ain't got no future.'

He smiled. 'That's nonsense. A girl with your talent has a very bright future.'

'No, you don't understand, sir ... '

'Yes I do, Lizzie. I know your people don't want you to go on to the village college.'

'It's mostly me dad, sir. Me mam would be OK with it I think.'

Mr Hardy sat down on the edge of his desk, one of his legs swinging.

'So,' he said. 'How can I persuade your dad to let you go on to secondary school and get some qualifications ... '

'I don't think you could do that, sir.'

Mr Hardy smiled. 'I could try. I could come down to the site and talk to him.'

'He's away working in Europe till the end of the summer.'

'Then I'll write to him.'

'He can't read much, sir. If he gets a letter, mostly he'll just tear it up.'

'Ah. I don't think it's something I can do over the phone.' He stroked his chin. 'Then I'll just wait till he gets back.'

'It'll be too late then.'

'Not necessarily, Lizzie. You can start on some home schooling and maybe I can get your dad to agree to you coming back at half term or something.'

'Maybe,' said Lizzie. But she knew it would be hopeless.

Mr Hardy folded his arms. 'What would you *really* like to do, Lizzie?'

Lizzie smiled. 'I'd like to make more jewellery,' she said. 'And I'd like to go to art college one day. But that's never gonna happen, is it?'

'Why not?'

'Well, for a start, it costs money to go to art college. And we haven't got that sort of money.'

'Don't give up on your dreams, Lizzie. There are grants, you know.'

'Grants?'

'Have you ever heard of the Prince's Trust?'

She shook her head.

'They give grants for all sorts of things. For setting up businesses, help with education, lots of things.'

'What, for the likes of me?'

'For exactly the likes of you.'

Lizzie looked up and smiled.

The bell rang and Mr Hardy stood up. 'Good luck, Lizzie,' he said.

Lizzie walked towards the door, then she stopped.

'Sir?'

'Yes.'

'There's this competition. An art competition. I thought I'd enter.'

Mr Hardy was gathering his books together. 'Good idea.'

'Only I have to give the address of my school.'

'Then put the address of the village college.'

'But I won't be there.'

'You put down the village college address and I promise you we'll work something out, even if your dad won't let you go next term.'

She and Tess gobbled their lunch. 'Was Mr Hardy very cross with you?' asked Tess.

'No, he was really helpful. He's a good bloke. He's gonna speak to me dad. He won't change his mind though.'

Eight

The last day of term was hard for Lizzie. Everyone was excited, talking about their plans for the holidays. Everyone, that is, except Lizzie – and some of the other traveller kids in Year Six.

At the end of the day she said goodbye to her friends and to some of the teachers.

None of them believe I won't be going on to the college.

'I've told the head of art there all about you,'

said Lizzie's art teacher. 'She's looking forward to having you there.'

Lizzie said nothing. What was the point?

'I'll come down and see Flame later,' said Tess.

Lizzie nodded. 'OK. I'll see you then.'

Back at the site, Lizzie leafed through her art project folder. She'd done a lot this term, good stuff, some of it. She put it away, sighing, then she walked down to the field. She hardly ever came to see the horses, but she needed to get away from the others on the site. Needed to clear her head.

She leant over the gate. No one else was there and she spent time looking around her, listening to the birdsong and squinting up at the sky. She could understand why her grandparents had loved to travel. New places, different people – and the freedom of being your own boss.

Mike appeared a little later. He nodded to her. 'Hi. You finished with school then?'

Lizzie shrugged. She couldn't be bothered to answer him.

He stood by the gate with her for a moment. 'You should stay on,' he said gruffly. 'It's a shame Dad's so set in his ways.'

Lizzie looked up, surprised. 'I didn't think you cared either way.'

Mike plucked a piece of grass and started chewing it. 'It's all changing, ain't it? You need a bit of paper, these days, to get anywhere.'

'I suppose I could make sommat of the jewellery.'

'Yeah. I s'pose.'

Lizzie changed the subject. 'Tess is coming down later. '

'Good. I've got summat to tell her.'

'Did you ask Dad about Flame?'

Mike sniffed. 'Yeah. He phoned last night. Wanted to know about the next fair, which horses we're taking.'

'What did he say – about Flame?'

Mike grinned. 'He wasn't keen at first, but I said we wouldn't have to pay nothing for her keep at the stables.'

'Is that true?'

'It'll have to be. If Tess wants to keep her over there, she'll have to sort it out.'

Just then, Tess came round the corner.

Lizzie smiled. 'Good news. Me dad says you can take Flame over to the riding stables.'

'Yesss' Tess punched the air.

'We're not paying nothing for her training,' said Mike quickly.

'No need,' said Tess. 'I've sorted it. I'm going to help there all holidays for nothing. In return, Angie's going to give me lessons.'

Lizzie stayed with them for a bit, but all the talk about horses bored her and she wandered back up to the site. At the entrance she hesitated, then instead of going to their plot, she walked down to the other end, where Lala lived.

Lala was out at work, but her mum was there. She was talking on the phone when Lizzie arrived, but she smiled at her and gestured for her to sit down on the van's steps.

At last, she finished her call. 'It never stops,' she said.

'What?'

'Fighting, Lizzie. Fighting for gypsies' rights.'

'What's happening now?'

Her auntie frowned. 'Some council wanting to throw two women off a field down in Sussex. One sick old woman and another single mother with a lot of kids. They're only there so they can be close to their family and there's no room for them on the site.'

'It's good of you to do all this. And for strangers, too.'

'They're our people, though.'

Her auntie came and sat down beside her. 'You finished school for the summer, Lizzie?'

'For ever,' said Lizzie.

'Umm,' said her auntie. 'You going to have the home schooling then?'

'Looks like it.'

'It's a pity you aren't staying on.'

Lizzie picked up a pebble from the ground and turned it over in her hands. 'Lala did all right, didn't she, with the home schooling?'

Her auntie nodded. 'If I'd had my way, Lala would have gone all through school.' she said grimly. 'But she was bullied and she got too scared to go back.' She hesitated. 'And all that trouble with her dad upset her, too.'

Lizzie didn't answer. Lala's dad had left her auntie. Mam always said he was a bully and a waster.

'The woman from the council's gonna come round after the holidays. There's some home education pack or something.'

Her auntie nodded. 'If you can't go on to the village college, Lizzie, I'll help you. Just like I helped Lala.'

Lizzie smiled. 'Would you do that for me?'

''Course I would.'

Lizzie went back to find Mam, who was making tea for the little ones in the kitchen of the day room. Mam didn't see her approach and Lizzie stood at the door for a moment, looking in. Her mam looked so tired, her hair loose and straggling down her back, and when she turned round Lizzie saw that there were beads of sweat on her forehead.

'Hello love. Holiday time now, eh?' The talking made her cough.

'Yeah,' said Lizzie bleakly. Mam turned back to the cooker, still coughing.

'You should stop smoking, Mam.'

The coughing fit took a while to subside. 'I know I should, love,' she said at last, wiping her eyes. The fags'll be the death of me.'

When Mam went off to work that evening, it seemed to Lizzie that the cough was worse.

'It's nothing,' she insisted, when Lizzie asked her again.

The next morning, Lizzie was up before her mam. She went to the van and peeped in. The little ones were out of bed, padding about in the van and they greeted Lizzie with hugs and shrieks. Lizzie opened the curtain that screened her parents' bed at the end of the van.

'Mam,' she said. 'You all right?'

'I'm not so good, love. Can you get the breakfast?' Her voice was croaky.

Lizzie never remembered her mam staying in bed. She felt a little stab of fear.

'I'll bring you some tea,' she said, ushering the kids out into the sunny morning and over to the day room. She gave them their breakfast and then took a cup of tea over to the van.

Her mam was sitting up in bed. She looked really poorly. And the cough was making her whole body shudder.

'It fair takes it out of me, this cough,' she admitted, sipping her tea.

'You can't go to work like this, Mam.'

'It'll be better by the evening.'

Lizzie shook her head. 'It won't Mam. It sounds really bad. You should phone in sick.'

Mam started coughing again. 'Don't fuss, Lizzie,' she spluttered.

Mam got up later in the day, but she felt so bad she had to go back to bed. And she let Lizzie phone her work to say she couldn't go in.

All during that night, Lizzie could hear her coughing in the van, and the kids crying. By the morning, Mam was worse. Lizzie's auntie came round and took the little ones back to hers. 'You best phone for the doctor, Lizzie,' she said.

'No,' said Mam, feebly. 'I don't need a doctor.'

'Don't be daft, girl,' said Auntie.

Lizzie pleaded. 'Summat's not right. Please let me get the doctor, Mam. There was that nice lady who came to see Nan. Maybe she would come round.'

'I just need to rest, love. I'll be fine.'

But the next day she was a lot worse and she was so weak that she didn't protest when Auntie said she'd phoned the clinic and asked for a lady doctor.

When the doctor finally came, it wasn't the lady who had treated Nan but a rather nervous young woman.

'Don't worry love,' said Auntie. 'We won't bite.'

The young doctor smiled weakly. She spent a long time examining Mam while Auntie, Lizzie and the kids all crowded outside, waiting to hear what she said.

When the doctor came out, she looked at Auntie. 'She's very poorly. I'm afraid she has pneumonia and she needs to be in hospital.

There was a shocked silence. Pneumonia was an illness they knew about. In the old times, especially in the winter, gypsy babies and old people had often died from pneumonia.

'I'll call an ambulance,' said the doctor, reaching for her phone.

Auntie cleared her throat. 'I'll go up the hospital with her.'

'I want to come, too,' said Lizzie.

'Yes,' said Auntie. 'You should be there. I'll go and fetch someone to mind the young 'uns.'

'And someone tell Mike his mam's took bad. He may want to come up the hospital later.'

The little ones cried when their mam was loaded into the ambulance. Lizzie bit her lip. 'You be good while I'm gone, d'you hear? I'll be back to make your tea.'

Then she climbed into the ambulance after Auntie.

Nine

The next few days were horrible. Lizzie spent most of her time at the hospital and other relations came and went. Once one of the nurses asked if less of them could come.

'It's difficult for us to do our work with all of you getting in our way,' she said.

Auntie folded her arms. 'We're family,' she said. 'She needs us.'

She turned to Lizzie. 'Silly chit of a girl,' she said. 'If the hospital weren't so near, she'd have the whole family camping in their vans in the car park.'

Lizzie nodded. She remembered a time when they'd lived on the other site, miles from a town, and whole families had set up their vans in the hospital car park when one of the children was taken bad.

On the day Lizzie's mam was taken to the hospital, Auntie phoned Dad, but it wasn't until the evening that she managed to get through to him. He and Auntie had never got on; she was the only woman in the family who challenged him. He asked to speak to Lizzie.

'What's happened to your mam, Lizzie?'

'She's really bad, Dad.' Hearing her dad's voice, Lizzie felt the tears coming to her eyes and her voice broke up. 'It's horrible seeing her like this. Her breathing's all funny and there's tubes everywhere.'

'Are they caring for her well?'

'Yeah. The doctors are great. And they explain everything to us.'

There was a long silence. Lizzie listened carefully. Her dad was struggling to control his tears. She couldn't believe it.

At last he said, 'I'm coming home, Lizzie.'

'But the job … '

'Never mind that, Lizzie. I need to be there with your mam.'

Lizzie switched off the phone and turned to Auntie. 'Dad's coming home,' she said.

Auntie nodded. 'I knew he would. He's got some daft ideas, your dad, but he's a true gypsy. Family comes first.'

It was true. When bad things happened, you could always turn to your family. At the site, everyone had rallied round. The other relations were caring for the little ones so Lizzie could be with her mam.

Lizzie and Auntie spent a lot of time together at the hospital, and although they were really worried about Mam, they spoke about other things, too.

One time, when they were sitting outside the ward, in the passage, drinking coffee from the machine there, Lizzie said. 'You went to secondary school, didn't you?'

Auntie blew on her coffee to cool it. 'I did, Lizzie, but it weren't without a fight.'

'Did your dad want you to stay home?'

'No, me dad was all for it. It was me mam. She'd had no learning and she wanted me to be like her. She wanted me to help her round the place and then they'd find me a nice gypsy boy to marry.'

Lizzie said nothing, and Auntie went on. 'But that didn't work out. I thought I knew best. I thought I was better than them, with my GCSEs and that. And I wouldn't look at the boys they wanted for me. I wanted to choose me own husband.'

Lizzie had never heard much about Auntie's husband. 'You married out, didn't you?'

'Yeah. And it were difficult, Lizzie. It works for some, but it didn't work for me. He couldn't understand how we were. How important family is to us. He was awkward, surrounded with our people.'

She sighed and took a sip of her coffee. 'And all his friends knew I was a gypsy – well, I never made a secret of it, like some of those who marry out – and they never really accepted me. And then I started campaigning for gypsy rights.'

'I think it's great what you do,' said Lizzie. Then she continued. 'So, if you went on to secondary school, why didn't Lala?'

Auntie frowned and Lizzie wondered if she'd gone too far.

'Lala had a hard time at school,' she said. 'Because of what I did. I was often in the local papers. Me husband's family hated it and we had ever so many rows. Then Lala was bullied at school and it was all because of me.'

'So you took her out?'

Auntie nodded. 'She wasn't learning anything. Every day I had a battle to get her to go to school. So I taught her myself; I went the home schooling route.'

Auntie shifted in her seat and gulped the rest of her coffee. 'And she did OK. She's happy and she's got a good job.'

'But you had the schooling to help her.'

'Yeah. And, like I said, I'll help you and all, Lizzie, if that's what you want.

'Mam can't help me.'

'I know. It's not her fault.'

Thinking about how hard Mam had worked all her life made Lizzie want to cry again, but she fought back the tears.

'She's not going to die, is she?'

Auntie put a hand on Lizzie's knee. 'She's a fighter, love. And she's got everything to live for. She's got great kids – you and Mike and the little ones. And, for all his faults, your dad's a good husband to her.'

The next day, Lizzie's dad turned up. He went straight to the hospital. Lizzie was on her own, sitting beside her mam. He touched her cheek briefly before sitting down on the other side of the bed. He took Mam's hand and talked to her softly, using some of the Roma language. Words they only used when they spoke to each other.

Mam had been asleep; she was asleep a lot of the time. But she opened her eyes when she heard his voice and smiled at him.

Lizzie looked at her dad. Tears were running down his cheeks.

Quietly, she got up and walked out of the ward.

Later, she and her dad drove back to the site. Lizzie glanced at him, hunched over the wheel of the truck, his face pale and lined with tiredness.

'When she saw you, Dad,' said Lizzie. 'That's the first time she's smiled.'

Dad sniffed. 'She's real poorly, ain't she?'

Lizzie nodded. She didn't trust herself to speak.

'You're a good girl, Lizzie.'

She raised her head, surprised. Dad never praised her. She didn't know what to say.

'You bin looking after the little 'uns?'

She nodded. 'Me and the others. Everyone's helped.'

They were all there to greet them when they got back to the site. Dad talked to the other men and to Mike, and he let the little ones cling onto him, not being impatient, as he sometimes was.

Auntie was there, too. He nodded at her. 'Thanks for your help,' he said.

In the evening, he went with Mike to look at the horses. Tess came up to the van.

'I didn't like to stay down there. I felt in the way. Your dad wanted to talk to Mike about stuff,' she said. 'I'd just come to tell Mike how Flame was getting on.'

Lizzie was trying to make some more jewellery, but her heart wasn't in it and she found it difficult to concentrate. She looked up from her work.

'Did he say anything. About Mam?'

Tess shook her head. 'It was all about the horses.' She hesitated. 'I told him about Flame and he seemed OK about it.'

Lizzie nodded.

Tess sat down beside her. 'How's your mam, Lizzie. Did you see her today?'

'Yeah. I was at the hospital when Dad turned up.' She sat back, giving up on threading beads. 'She smiled at him.'

'Oh Lizzie! That's good, isn't it?'

Lizzie bit her lip. 'I hope so. She's not done any smiling before.'

Tess looked round the van. 'The van looks great. Are you keeping it clean for her?'

'It's summat I can do,' said Lizzie. 'All the aunties are looking after the kids. At least I can keep the van clean.'

They sat in silence for a while, then Tess cleared her throat. 'Have you talked to your dad about going on to the village college?'

'He can't think about that now, Tess.'

Tess picked up a bead and held it to the light. 'No, I suppose not, but now he's home, maybe Mr Hardy could come and see him?'

'Leave it, Tess. It's not important.' Lizzie's eyes flashed with anger. 'Nothing's so important as me family. All we want is for Mam to pull through.'

'I'm sorry. I didn't mean ... '

Lizzie put her head in her hands. 'I can't think about anything else. I just want me mam back.'

Ten

The days dragged on. Lizzie went nowhere except up to the hospital or round the site. All her aunties and uncles and cousins were helping out when they could.

One day, Dad came back from the hospital. He found Lizzie talking to a group of her girl cousins.

'She's coming home!' he said, a huge smile on his face.

'Mam's coming home? That's great. When?'

'Next week. They've said she can come home as long as she rests.'

'We'll make sure she does,' said Lizzie.

Lizzie didn't even think of asking her dad about staying on at school. Right now, that seemed even more impossible. Mam was going to need care and she wouldn't be able to look after the kids or go out to work for a while.

When Mam came back to the site, she was still pale and very thin, but as soon as she saw the van, she grinned. 'Oh, it's good to be home,' she said. 'And it's all so clean and tidy.' She looked round at the gleaming chrome and the spotless windows. 'You've done ever so well.'

Lizzie smiled. 'See, Mam, we can do all the chores. Don't worry about anything. You just get better.'

As time went by Mam got stronger and started to take an interest in things about her.

'What about your jewellery, Lizzie?' she asked one day. 'You should get going with that. Summer's the time to sell it – at car boots and fêtes and that.'

Lizzie shrugged. 'Yeah. I know.' But the truth was she couldn't get keen on it again. Mam's illness had scared her and sapped her energy. She felt listless and the future loomed dull ahead of her. She'd never do anything with the jewellery, and even if her auntie helped her, she was sure she'd never go back to school or on to art college.

Tess came to see her a few times during the holidays and tried to cheer her up, but even she couldn't lift her spirits.

'Flame's coming on really well, Lizzie. Why don't you come down to the riding school and watch us?'

Lizze shook her head. 'No. I'd best stay here.'

'Lizzie!' said Tess. 'What's happened to you?'

'I dunno. I guess I'm just a gypsy girl and I'll stay here and help round the place.'

Auntie came round and spoke to her. 'It's bin a shock, love, seeing your mam so ill, but you must think of yourself now, think of your future.'

'What future?'

Auntie took Lizzie's shoulders and shook her. 'What we spoke about, Lizzie. I'm gonna help you with your home schooling, like we said.'

'Thanks,' said Lizzie, but there was no enthusiasm in her voice. She was grateful to Auntie, but it wouldn't be the same as being at school with her friends, being able to work in the art room.

Mam noticed the difference in her, too. 'All the spark's gone out of you, Lizzie. What's the matter?'

But Lizzie only shrugged again.

'Come on,' said Mam. 'Get out your beads and glass baubles. I'll help you.'

'I don't feel like it ... '

'Well I'll do it, then,' said Mam, and she got all the stuff from the drawers and put it on the table. Lizzie watched her try and match up beads and thread them. She wasn't bad at it, but it wasn't how Lizzie would have done it, and after a while she picked up a piece of wire and started matching up pieces from the table. Mam said nothing and went on working. When she had finished threading a necklace, she held it up.

'Not bad, eh?'

Lizzie smiled. 'Not great, Mam!'

She took the necklace and changed it. 'There. That's better.'

'Now, why didn't I think of that!'

They worked on together for the rest of the afternoon. The kids were all happy playing with their cousins outside and the sun streamed through the windows, making the pieces of jewellery sparkle.

By the evening, they'd made several new pieces between them.

'There's the village fête next week,' said Mam. 'You could try selling them there. It'd be good to get some money in.'

Lizzie looked at her. 'Are you worried about money?'

Mam put down the piece she was working on. 'I shouldn't have said that.'

But Lizzie knew it was true. Dad hadn't been working since he got back. He'd been training up the horses to the trotting carts and going to the pub with the other men. And Mam hadn't been able to go back to work.

When Tess came round the next evening, she found Lizzie hard at work.

'Hey. It's good to see you doing this again.'

'I reckon someone's got to earn some money in this family,' muttered Lizzie.

Tess frowned. 'What about benefits? Surely your mam could claim, couldn't she?'

'We've never taken nothing off the state,' said Lizzie. 'We don't hold with that. Though there's some gypsy families who don't bother working and they just live on the benefits. But me dad's always said we don't want no favours. We want to be free and earn our own money.' Anyway,' she went on 'it's that hard to claim. There's forms and that.'

Tess had her hands on the table. She picked up one of the pieces and it lay idly in the palm of her hand.

Lizzie looked at Tess's hand and then looked quickly away.

'What?'

'Nothing.'

'Have you seen something? You can read palms, can't you Lizzie?'

'No. I never said I could ... '

'You did, so. You said you had the gift, like your little nan.'

Lizzie didn't answer.

'What did you see, Lizzie? Was it something bad?'

Lizzie smiled and took Tess's hand. She removed the piece of jewellery from it and examined the lines.

'I can't see anything but good for you, Tess,' she said. 'Everything'll turn out great.'

Tess frowned. 'You sure?'

''Course I'm sure.'

But she wouldn't look Tess in the eye.

Lizzie took a stall at the village fête and, once again,

her jewellery sold out. There were some disappointed customers, too.

'I can make some more,' said Lizzie, and she found herself taking orders.

'I'll have to have a deposit,' she said firmly. 'I have to buy the beads and stuff.'

Tess was at the fête, too. Lizzie saw her talking to a fair-haired boy.

'Was that your brother?' asked Lizzie, when Tess came back. 'The one Mike had the fight with?'

'Yeah, that's Ben. He thinks he's gonna be a football star! Stupid boys, who needs them?'

Lizzie grinned.

Later that day, when she was counting out the money, she found the crumpled poster about the art competition. She smoothed it out and looked at it again. At the bottom was an entry form. She read it slowly then sat staring at it.

Maybe she would enter the competition.

There was no harm in trying, was there?

You had to put the name of your school and the head of art. Carefully she wrote the address of the village college and of the head of the Art Department. She knew her name, her art teacher at the primary school had told her.

When she finished filling in the form, she found

the paints that Tess had given her for Christmas and the pad of paper and started work. She knew exactly the picture she wanted to paint. It was all in her head and it was as if her little nan was beside her, guiding her.

As she worked, she could almost smell the smoke, see the colourful vardo and Nan's family sitting around the open fire. She drew someone playing the fiddle, some of the women working on paper flowers and a group of horses tethered nearby.

She sat up late into the night working on the painting, putting more and more detail into it. She was glad she had her own room in the shed on their plot. This way, the painting could be her secret. She wouldn't tell anyone about it – not even Mam or Tess – and tomorrow she'd go to the post office in the village, buy a big envelope and send it off.

The next morning she looked at the painting in daylight. And then she saw that there was a space on the entry form for a title. She frowned, chewing the end of her biro. Then she wrote, in big capital letters:

GYPSY LIFE

She stretched and yawned, then she got dressed and set off for the village. She took some time choosing a big padded envelope and then she put the poster inside, sealed the envelope and addressed, stamped and posted it.

When she'd finished, she walked slowly back to the site; but just before she got there, she stopped and looked up to the sky.

'It's for you, Nan.'

And suddenly she heard a skylark, way above her, singing its heart out.

The Travellers
Four people, one story

Rosemary Hayes lives in Cambridgeshire with her husband and an assortment of animals. She worked for Cambridge University Press and then for some years she ran her own publishing company, Anglia Young Books. Rosemary has written over forty books for children in a variety of genres and for a variety of age groups, many of which have been shortlisted for awards.

Rosemary is also a reader for a well known authors' advisory service and she runs creative writing workshops for both children and adults.

To find out more about Rosemary, visit her website: *www.rosemaryhayes.co.uk*

Follow her on twitter: *@HayesRosemary*

Read her blog at *www.rosemaryhayes.co.uk/wpf*